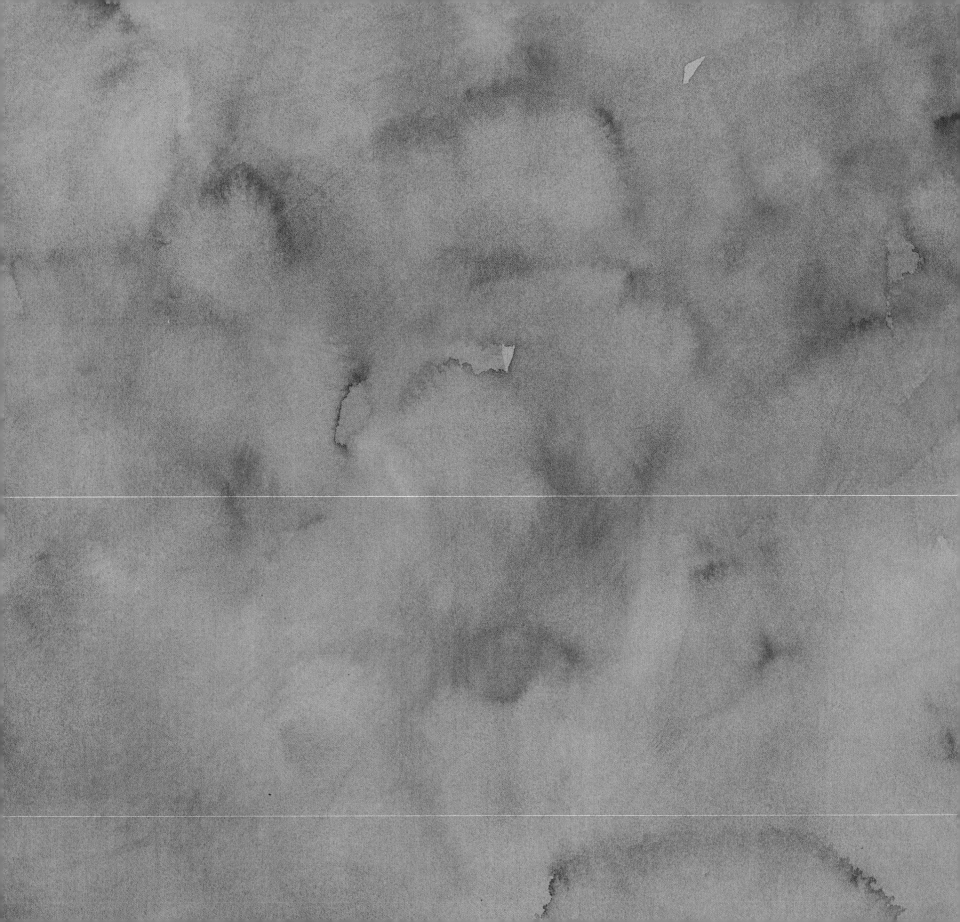

...ll We Need

illustrated by

Kathy Wolff

Margaux Meganck

BLOOMSBURY
CHILDREN'S BOOKS
NEW YORK LONDON OXFORD NEW DELHI SYDNEY

BLOOMSBURY CHILDREN'S BOOKS
Bloomsbury Publishing Inc., part of Bloomsbury Publishing Plc
1385 Broadway, New York, NY 10018

BLOOMSBURY, BLOOMSBURY CHILDREN'S BOOKS, and the Diana logo are trademarks of Bloomsbury Publishing Plc

First published in the United States of America in June 2021
by Bloomsbury Children's Books

Bloomsbury books may be purchased for business or promotional use. For information on bulk purchases please contact
Macmillan Corporate and Premium Sales Department at specialmarkets@macmillan.com

Library of Congress Cataloging-in-Publication Data
Names: Wolff, Kathy, author. | Meganck, Margaux, illustrator.
Title: All we need / by Kathy Wolff ; illustrated by Margaux Meganck.
Description: New York : Bloomsbury Children's Books, 2021.
Summary: Illustrations and easy-to-read, rhyming text celebrate the littlest things one needs to
be happy, and the beauty of sharing with others when one has more than enough.
Identifiers: LCCN 2020041149 (print) | LCCN 2020041150 (e-book)
ISBN 978-1-61963-874-7 (hardcover) • ISBN 978-1-61963-875-4 (e-book) • ISBN 978-1-61963-876-1 (e-PDF)
Subjects: CYAC: Basic needs—Fiction. | Contentment—Fiction. | Sharing—Fiction.
Classification: LCC PZ8.3.W8442 All 2021 (print) | LCC PZ8.3.W8442 (e-book) | DDC [E]—dc23
LC record available at https://lccn.loc.gov/2020041149

The art for this book was created using watercolor, gouache, and colored pencil on watercolor paper
Typeset in Oranda BT
Book design by Danielle Ceccolini
Printed in China by Leo Paper Products, Heshan, Guangdong
2 4 6 8 10 9 7 5 3 1

All papers used by Bloomsbury Publishing Plc are natural, recyclable products made from wood grown in well-managed forests.
The manufacturing processes conform to the environmental regulations of the country of origin.

To find out more about our authors and books visit www.bloomsbury.com and sign up for our newsletters.

For Bill, who's a very important
part of all I need —K. W.

To my parents, who have always ensured that
I have all I need. Thank you. Love, MB —M. M.

All we need
is what's found in the breeze,
in the stillness of nothing, in the rustle of trees,
when we take a deep breath, what's not *seen*—but is *there* . . .

All we need . . .

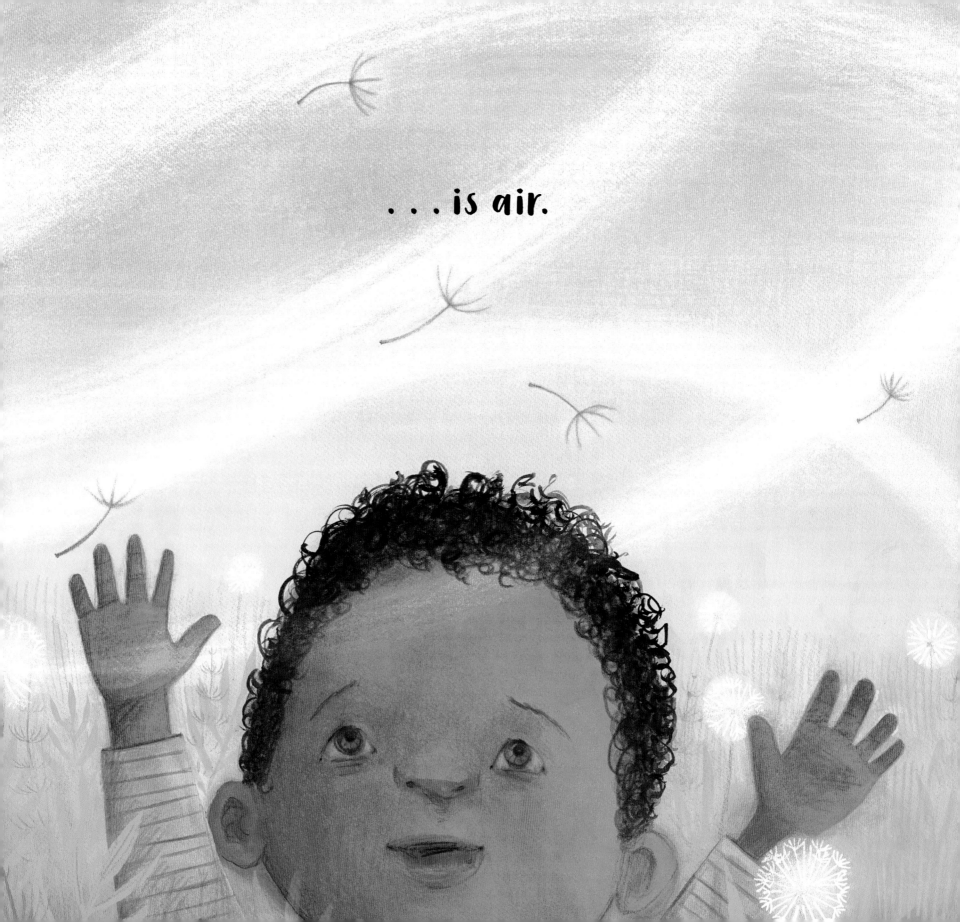

. . . is air.

All we need
is what falls from above
to fill up our glass and our bucket and tub,
to drink to feel cool, to splash when it's hotter . . .

All we need . . .

. . . is water.

All we need

may be found in a book,

in a welcoming classroom, or a curious look.

We can try and may fail, but we'll gain in return . . .

All we need . . .

. . . is to learn.

All we need
is a roof overhead,
walls to surround us, a cover, a bed,
a place to feel safe, a place we feel known . . .

All we need . . .

. . . is a home.

All we need
is a belly that's filled,
to give us the strength to grow and rebuild.
Whether it's roasted or simmered or stewed . . .

All we need . . .

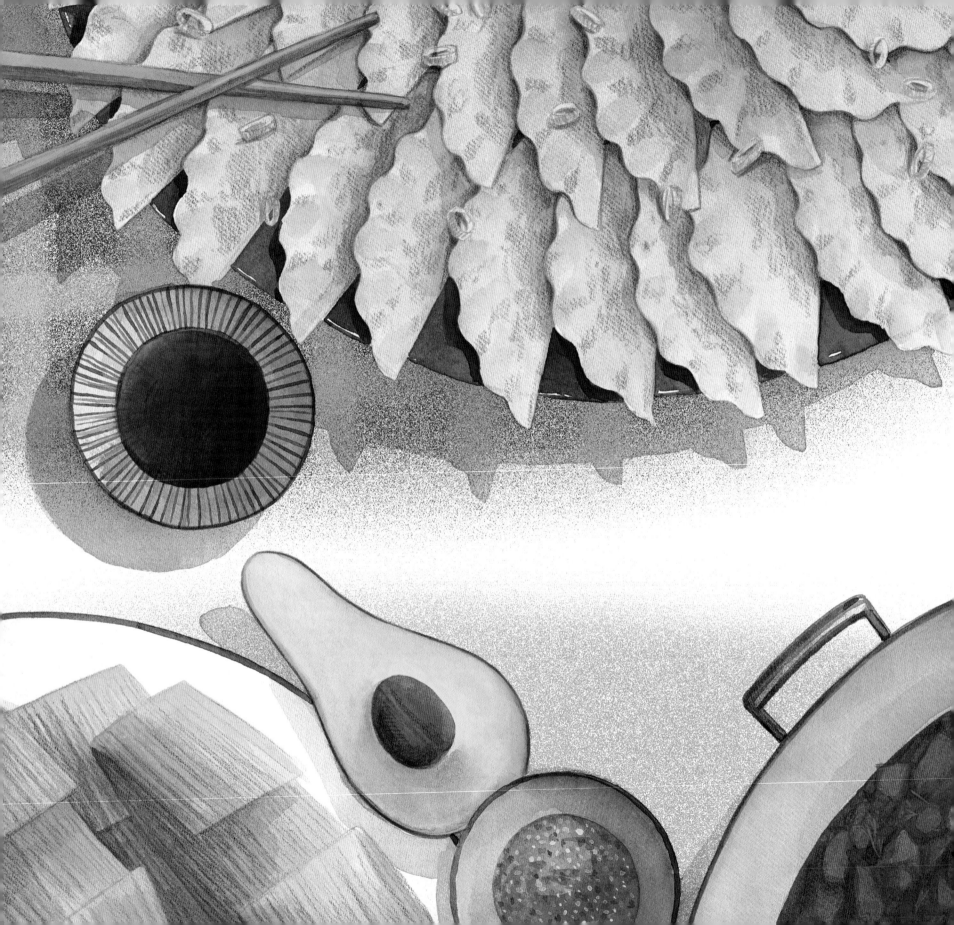

. . . is food.

All we need
is a hug and a smile,
a shoulder to lean on every once in a while,
the comfort of knowing that love never ends . . .

All we need . . .

. . . is our family and friends.

And when we have found that we *have* all of these,
when our cup trickles over, when we're well and at ease,
when we have all we need, plus a little to spare . . .

The only need left . . .

. . . is to share.

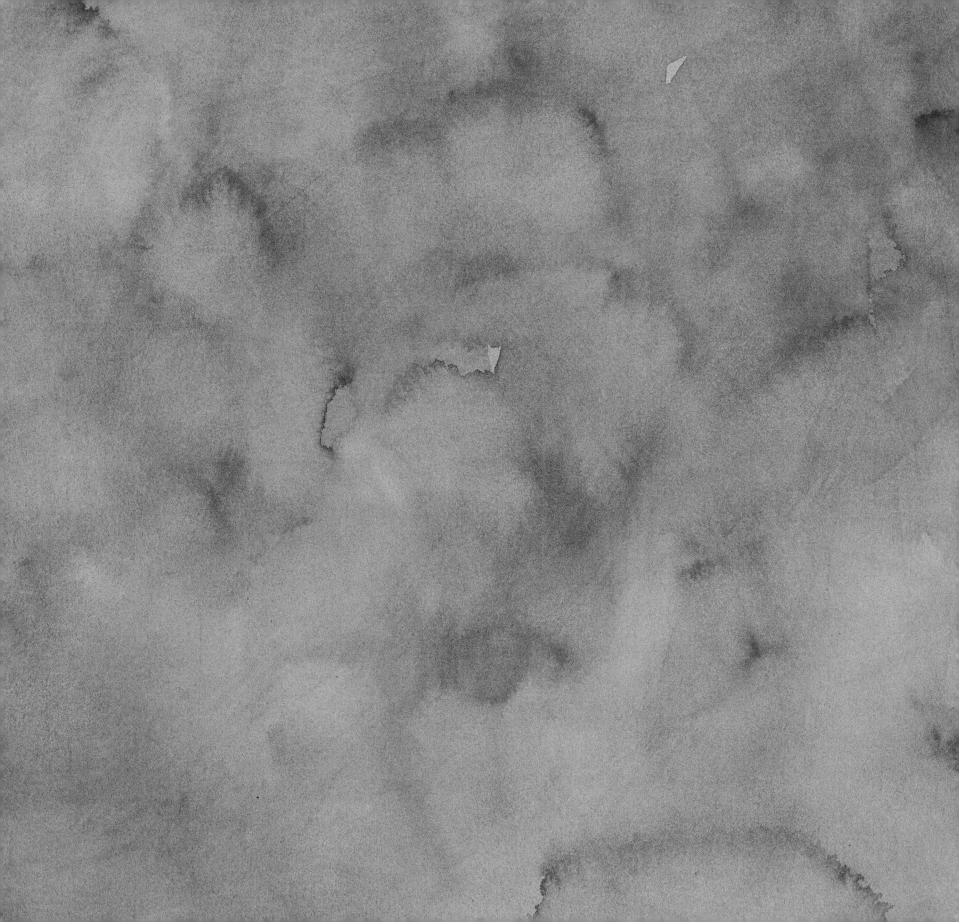